BUNNY
WILL NOT
JUMP!

**WRITTEN AND ILLUSTRATED
BY JASON THARP**

Ready-to-Read

Simon Spotlight
New York London Toronto Sydney New Delhi

SIMON SPOTLIGHT

An imprint of Simon & Schuster Children's Publishing Division

1230 Avenue of the Americas, New York, New York 10020

This Simon Spotlight edition December 2020

Copyright © 2020 by Jason Tharp
SIMON SPOTLIGHT, READY-TO-READ, and colophon are registered trademarks of Simon & Schuster, Inc.

For information about special discounts for bulk purchases, please contact Simon & Schuster Special Sales at 1-866-506-1949 or business@simonandschuster.com.

Manufactured in the United States of America 1020 LAK

10 9 8 7 6 5 4 3 2 1

This book has been cataloged with the Library of Congress.

ISBN 978-1-5344-8303-3 (hc)

ISBN 978-1-5344-8302-6 (pbk)

ISBN 978-1-5344-8304-0 (eBook)

He seems sad, too.

I just want him to be happy.

Maybe you can help!

It all started the other day. . . .

What is the point?
I will never be able to
jump like you.

I do not like prizes,
or lettuce!

Bunny still will not jump.

That is why I need your help.

Maybe if you shake the book,

Bunny will jump!

Ready? Okay!
Please shake the book
up and down . . .
now!

That made me dizzy, but it did not make me jump.

It did not work, but that is okay.

We can try again.

This is the Jump-O-Matic 4000.

It is a machine that will help Bunny jump.

I do not understand.

I am a bunny.

I should be the best

at jumping!

You are great at jumping.
I can jump higher and farther
because I am taller.
We are different,
and that is okay!

Come on, Bunny.

Do not think about how I jump.

Jump the best way YOU can jump!

**Flip the page back and forth
to help Bunny jump!** ➡